For my Big Love Kalea—

From your Gramma ☺

Always with all my Love—
♡ x x o x x ♡

Kaipo
& the
Mighty
'Ahi

Written and Illustrated by
Leonard J. Villanueva

BEACHHOUSE
Publishing, LLC

For Douglas

ISBN 0-9729905-6-9

Library of Congress Catalog Card Number: 2004103218

First Printing, June 2004
Second Printing, April 2005
2 3 4 5 6 7 8 9

BeachHouse Publishing, LLC
PO Box 2926
Ewa Beach, Hawai`i 96706
beachhousepub@hawaii.rr.com
www.beachhousepublishing.com

Printed in Korea

Mahalo to

Henry K. Iwasa, Executive Secretary, and Edith McKinzie, Chair
University of Hawai`i at Mānoa, School of Hawaiian, Asian and Pacific Studies (SHAPS),
Committee for the Preservation and Study of Hawaiian Language, Art and Culture

Honowai Elementary School—Faculty, Staff, Students, and Parents

My family—José, Judith, José Jr., Marjorie, Anthony, Elisa, Marc,
Linda, Laverne, Kenneth, David, and Frank

Wooden canoe paddles break the surface of the sea sending millions of tiny bubbles downward, then upward. The orange and red sunlight above shines on the swirling bubbles as the sun sets.

Three young men jump out of their canoe and drag it ashore. Their youngest brother, Kaipo, scurries down the beach to greet them. He looks into their canoe and then at their disappointed faces. Once again the brothers have returned without any fish.

"Tomorrow will be a better day," encourages Kaipo.

"Go away!" growls proud Ho'okano. "We're tired."

The brothers lumber past, moving their canoe toward the safety of its thatched hut. Kaipo follows them like a playful puppy.

"I can show you where all the fish are waiting to be caught," Kaipo says.

"We know where they are," Kānalua sighs. "We all had fish on our lines, but the fish snapped our lines and stole our hooks."

"Please take me with you next time," Kaipo pleads. "I will catch us a fine fish."

"Don't be silly, Kaipo. You are too small," snaps Ho'okano. "The deep water 'ahi is a mighty fish. It would pull you into the water and swallow you in one gulp."

The brothers laugh. The oldest brother, Akeake, musses Kaipo's hair and smiles.

Not discouraged, Kaipo takes a line and hook from inside the canoe and pretends to fish. He strains against an imaginary catch. "It is a fine fish. The mighty 'ahi will fight me, but I will not give in. It strains to break free, but I keep fighting. I pull and pull."

"You will have your chance one day, Kaipo," Akeake interrupts. He takes the line from Kaipo and begins to roll it up.

"When?" Kaipo asks hopefully. "When will I have my chance?"

"One day," promises Akeake. "Do not be in such a hurry to grow up. Many responsibilities await you then."

"Enough talking," grunts Kānalua. "We've got lots of work to do before the sun sinks completely into the sea."

They leave Kaipo standing on the beach, facing the wide ocean. Whispering waves wash over the now pink and purple sand. Kaipo's small silhouette slowly melts as the sky turns to black.

It is morning now. Long, black lashes blink slowly as Kaipo awakens. Beams of white morning sunlight pierce the walls of his family's thatched hut, and the familiar morning cry of the curlew soars above the beach. Kaipo half stretches before he realizes that the sun is already high in the sky. He jumps to his bare feet and races down the beach, kicking up clouds of powdery, white sand. He runs past his best friend, Pilialo, with just a quick smile and a wave. The brothers are already in the water with their canoe.

"Wait!" Kaipo squeals. "Take me with you!" He enters the water, tripping as he hits the whitewash. The brothers laugh at him. "Please take me with you. I will catch us a fine fish today." Like a sand crab, he quickly climbs aboard. "Oh, you will all catch fish today, but yours will not be as fine as mine."

"Ha!" Kānalua snorts, slightly irritated. "So you think you know where the fish are, do you? Well, maybe you can swim there."

The brothers toss the pesky sand crab overboard.

"Maybe the fish will come to you, Kaipo!" Ho'okano snickers.

The canoe pulls away. Kaipo picks seaweed out of his long black hair and scratches the fine wet sand out of his ears. His best friend, Pilialo, helps him up.

"Don't be angry with them, Kaipo," urges Pilialo. "They're just disappointed they haven't caught many fish this season. Besides, we are too young and no match against the powerful 'ahi."

"I will catch a mighty 'ahi one day," Kaipo vows. "And they will not laugh at me."

"Come, Kaipo, let's not concern ourselves with such things. The wind is picking up, and it looks like it's going to be a good day for flying our kites."

The two friends get their kites and head for their favorite spot high on a hill. Once at the top, the boys slowly let the playful breeze pull their kites into the morning sky. The cool blue ocean below mirrors the warm blue sky in front of them. They sit for a while.

"Pilialo, don't you hate being treated like a baby?" Kaipo asks.

"Oh, I like it," Pilialo jokes. "I don't have to work so hard."

"Be serious," Kaipo scolds. "Don't you sometimes feel stuck?"

"You mean like the time I was playing between those two trees and got my head trapped?" Pilialo laughs at himself.

Kaipo moans and rolls his eyes. "No, I mean stuck in what someone else thinks about you. I'm more than what people think I am. I'm always full of ideas. Full of questions. I am sunlight and thundercloud. I am Kaipo." His eyes scan the horizon. "Oh, never mind," he sighs. "I don't know what I mean."

Kaipo tosses a small pebble over the side of the hill and watches it dive toward the ocean far below. The boys sit in silence.

"Sometimes," Pilialo breaks the uneasy quiet, "sometimes late at night when everyone is asleep, I leave my mat and walk out on the beach. I stare up at the moon and imagine I'm a giant white bird. I soar up into the sky and look at everyone below. People look up at me and shout with pride, 'Hey, that's Pilialo!' Is that what you mean?"

"Yeah," Kaipo nods, "something like that."

The two friends exchange smiles and continue flying their kites.

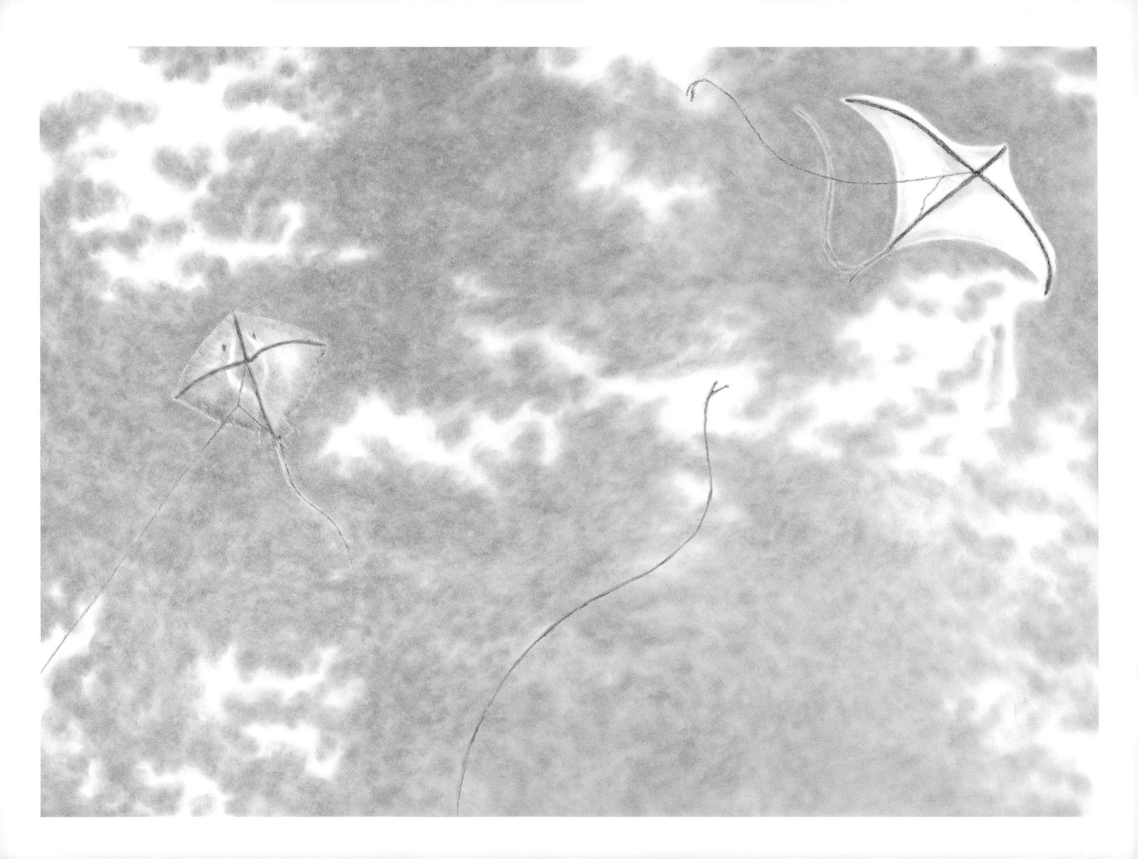

"The wind sure is strong," Kaipo says. "Let's give our kites lots of slack today."

The boys' kites are instantly pulled high into the sky by a sudden gust of wind. Without thinking, Pilialo tightens his grip on his string, and immediately his line snaps. "Oh, dog's fart! That's the third kite I've lost." Pilialo frowns as the wind takes his kite out to sea.

"That's what happens when you don't let the line out enough," Kaipo lectures. "Haven't you learned your lesson yet? If you don't let the line out when the wind is strong, the kite will snap its string and fly away." Kaipo is struck silent as a thought sneaks up on him. "Hey, that's it!"

"That's what?" asks Pilialo.

"That's it!" Kaipo exclaims. "Watch what happens when I fight my kite." Kaipo allows a powerful gust of wind to quickly take his kite high into the sky. He immediately tightens his grip on the string, and—snap!—the kite breaks free of its leash. "See!" Kaipo says joyfully. "You lose your kite if you don't let the line out! Isn't that wonderful?"

Pilialo scratches one of his eyebrows, confused. "I don't see why you're so happy. Now we've both lost our kites."

"You'll see," Kaipo says as he scampers down the side of the hill, heading toward his hut.

"Hey, wait!" Pilialo yelps. "What about our kites?"

"Never mind the kites," Kaipo hollers back. "I've got a fish to catch!"

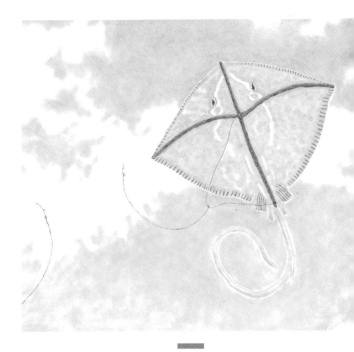

A few hours later, Kaipo sits on the sand with all the fishing gear he could find. As his brothers' canoe approaches the beach, he jumps to his feet. He has gathered much more equipment than is required. Fishing lines drape from each tanned arm; fishing hooks of various sizes hang from his neck; gourds filled with drinking water balance on his narrow shoulders; and a bunch of bananas tied to his waist chases him as he scrambles down the beach.

The brothers jump out of their canoe and into the shallow water. Kaipo staggers up to meet them, weary under the heavy load.

"Look at what the tide dragged in," Ho'okano snickers.

"Here we go again," warns Kānalua.

"Wait! We've got to go back out!" cries Kaipo. "Put your canoe back in the water. We've got to go back out!"

"What do you mean 'we'? We are not going anywhere. We are tired," Kānalua groans. "Our lines are broken, and the mighty 'ahi has taken most of our hooks."

"Just go away, Kaipo," Ho'okano barks. "We don't have time for any of your nonsense."

"Please! The sun is still high enough in the sky to try again. I know the mighty 'ahi has been snapping your lines and taking your hooks. But I know how to beat it."

"And we know how to beat you," Ho'okano threatens. "Now go away before we bury you neck deep in the sand."

"How do you know anything, Kaipo?" questions Kānalua. "Why don't you go play with Pilialo?"

Kaipo gives a pleading look at his oldest brother. "Please, Akeake, you've got to give me a chance. I'm ready for responsibility. I know I can help. Please let me try."

"Okay, Kaipo," Akeake yields. "We'll give you one chance to prove what you know."

"What!" Kānalua roars. "Are you joking? He doesn't know the first thing about fishing. Look here — he has bananas! That's bad luck on a fishing journey."

"He'll leave the bananas," interrupts Akeake. "He can show us how to catch the mighty `ahi if he promises to never bother us again."

"I promise," Kaipo agrees, still struggling under the weight of his load.

The brothers look at the pitiful sight and then at each other. They turn the canoe around and push it back into the water. Kaipo climbs aboard and his brothers help him with his gear.

The young men paddle their tiny canoe out to sea. When they reach a spot where they believe they can find `ahi, the brothers slow their pace.

"Okay, Kaipo, what's the secret?" asks Kānalua.

"Drop your hooks here," he directs. "And wait for the fish to bite."

"We already know that part," snickers Ho'okano. "Tell us something new."

"Shh! Quiet." Akeake whispers. "Hold steady, Kaipo. The hungry 'ahi will soon take the whole hook."

Suddenly, Kaipo's line is pulled from his hands. The mighty 'ahi bites the hook and takes off with lightning speed. The great fish heads straight down, far below the small canoe, back towards its school. A thin line of smoke rises from the spot where Kaipo's whizzing line rubs against the side of the canoe. The brothers quickly jump to help Kaipo regain control of the line.

"No!" Kaipo stops them. "Let the 'ahi take the line! Let it take the line."

"But you'll let the fish get away," Kānalua yells.

"It won't get away," Kaipo argues. "You have to let the line out if you don't want it to snap. You have to let the line out!"

"Listen to Kaipo," Akeake says. "Let the line out."

Kaipo's fishing line is taken far from the canoe as the brothers watch anxiously. Soon the weight of the line's great length begins to wear on the determined `ahi. The line slows its pace. Kaipo takes hold of it.

"We still have the `ahi," Kaipo smiles.

"Okay," Akeake says, "start paddling."

The brothers obey. Kaipo picks up a paddle while Akeake steadily pulls the line in.

"Do you still have the fish?" Ho`okano asks.

"Yes, we've still got it," Akeake shouts over his shoulder. "Keep paddling!"

The young men laugh excitedly as they continue paddling with all their strength. Millions of tiny bubbles are pushed downward, then upward as their wooden paddles break the surface of the water. Akeake continues to retrieve the great length of fishing line. His muscles strain against the weight of the fish.

"I'll need some help soon," Akeake says. "This is going to be a great fish."

Kaipo puts down his paddle. With a final heave, Kaipo helps Akeake pull the mighty ʻahi into their canoe. The brothers rejoice at their success. They continue fishing using Kaipo's advice, letting out the line and retrieving it once the fish grow weary. The brothers take turns pulling up many beautiful ʻahi. With their magnificent catch, they finally head home.

The satisfied sun starts to set as the canoe and men approach the shore. Tired, but happy, Kānalua declares, "We caught some fine fish, didn't we?"

"Yes," Ho`okano agrees proudly, "some fine fish."

"Kaipo," Akeake smiles, "don't forget your line and hook. You'll need them the next time we go out."

About the Author

Leonard Villanueva grew up in Pearl City as one of eleven children. For generations, his family fished treasures from the sea, catching marlin, pāpio, ulua, akule, and āholehole. Although not himself a fisherman, Villanueva felt drawn to write a story that celebrated Hawai'i's youth—their creativity, perseverance, and loyalty to family.

Nicknamed "Mr. Standards" by his principal and colleagues at Honowai Elementary School, Villanueva was awarded the Milken Family Foundation National Educator Award in 2002. As an artist and fifth grade teacher, Villanueva created a program called "Art All Day, Everyday" which allows students to meet standards through art.

He currently lives in Pearl City with his son Douglas. This is his first children's book.